SPORTS SUPERSTARS

LEBRON JAMES

By Anthony K. Hewson

Kaleidoscope
Minneapolis, MN

Your Front Row Seat to the Games

This edition is co-published by agreement between Kaleidoscope and World Book, Inc.

Kaleidoscope Publishing, Inc.
6012 Blue Circle Drive
Minnetonka, MN 55343 U.S.A.

World Book, Inc.
180 North LaSalle St., Suite 900
Chicago IL 60601 U.S.A.

Kaleidoscope ISBNs
978-1-64519-041-7 (library bound)
978-1-64494-198-0 (paperback)
978-1-64519-142-1 (ebook)

World Book ISBN
978-0-7166-4344-9 (library bound)

Library of Congress Control Number
2019940060

Printed in the United States of America.

TABLE OF CONTENTS

CHAPTER 1

Bringing It Home

LeBron James rises up for a three-point shot. A defender reaches to stop him. But James keeps his focus. The ball drops through the hoop. Swish! James scores his first three-pointer of the game.

It's Game 7 of the 2016 National Basketball Association (NBA) Finals. James's Cleveland Cavaliers are playing the Golden State Warriors. The winner of this game takes home the championship. James's basket puts Cleveland ahead 89–87. But the game isn't done yet. Less than five minutes remain. That's plenty of time for Golden State. The Warriors are the defending champions.

FUN FACT
James selected jersey No. 23 in honor of Michael Jordan.

LeBron James goes up for a basket in Game 7 of the 2016 NBA Finals.

James rises up to smack away Andre Iguodala's shot.

One shot misses. Then another. Neither team can take control. With two minutes left, the teams are tied 89–89.

Then Cleveland misses again. The Warriors get the **rebound**. Guard Andre Iguodala dribbles quickly up the floor. He cuts to the basket for a layup. It looks like it will be an easy basket. Not so fast. James bursts down the court. Seemingly out of nowhere, he leaps into the air. Then he smacks the ball off the **backboard**. No one can believe it. James's blocked shot stopped a basket. And now Cleveland has the ball again.

CLASH OF THE TITANS

Golden State beat Cleveland in the 2015 NBA Finals. The Warriors were even better in 2015–16. In fact, they were one of the best teams ever. They won 73 regular-season games. That set a new record. They dominated thanks to their amazing three-point shooting.

Where James Has Been

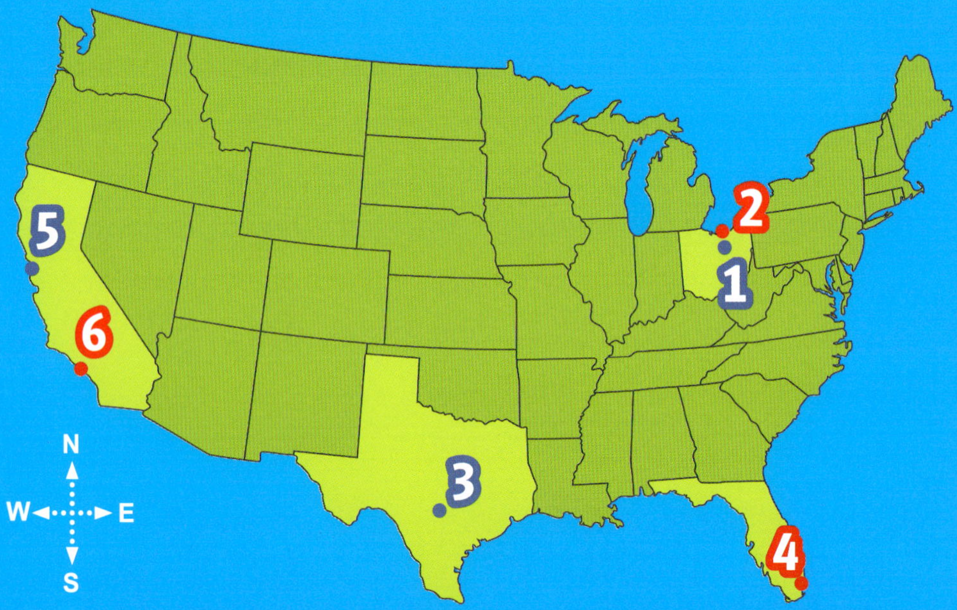

1 **Akron, Ohio:** James was born here.

2 **Cleveland, Ohio:** Home of the Cavaliers, who selected James in the 2003 NBA **Draft**.

3 **San Antonio, Texas:** James played in his first NBA Finals game against the Spurs in 2007.

4 **Miami, Florida:** James won NBA championships in 2012 and 2013 while playing for the Heat.

5 **Oakland, California:** James led the Cavaliers to a win in the 2016 NBA Finals, where they beat Golden State on the road in Game 7 to clinch Cleveland's first major sports championship in 52 years.

6 **Los Angeles, California:** James began playing with the Lakers in 2018.

FUN FACT

The Cavaliers were the first team to come back from being down 3–1 in an NBA Finals series.

The 2016 NBA title was an emotional one for James and many other Ohio natives.

Both teams miss a shot. Then the Cavaliers hit a three-pointer. It puts them up 92–89. Soon James gets the ball back once again. He is ready to take control. He gets up into the air to go for a dunk. But a defender hits him hard. James falls to the ground. He's slow in getting up. He makes just one of two **free throws**. But that is enough. Cleveland wins 93–89.

James celebrates with teammates. He even begins to cry. Cleveland had not won a major championship since 1964. James wanted to end that streak. And he did it against one of the best teams in NBA history.

CHAPTER 2

A Young Star

LeBron James flies up toward the basket. He grabs the pass out of the air. Then he slams the ball down through the hoop. Thousands of fans stand and cheer. One of them is famous rapper Jay-Z. They are all there to see this 18-year-old.

It was March 2003. LeBron was playing in the McDonald's All-American Game. It's a big game. Only the best high school players in the country are invited. Many go on to reach the NBA. The 2003 All-American Game was extra special. That's because LeBron was already a big star.

FUN FACT

Many people around the country first learned of LeBron when he was in eighth grade. He led his team to the finals of a national basketball tournament that year.

LeBron goes up for a shot during the 2003 McDonald's All-American Game.

FUN FACT

Top college football programs such as Notre Dame wanted LeBron to play football for them.

Akron is the fifth largest city in Ohio.

LeBron was born on December 30, 1984, in Akron, Ohio. His early life was hard. He was an only child. His mother raised him by herself. They never had much money. This forced them to move a lot. And often their neighborhoods were not very safe. LeBron tried to avoid the dangers. He spent a lot of time shooting hoops at a local park.

In fifth grade, LeBron began playing organized sports. He joined football and basketball teams. Even then, his athletic talents were easy to see. Dru Joyce coached a local high school basketball team. He brought LeBron to play for him at St. Vincent-St. Mary's High School.

LeBron joined the football team. He became a star wide receiver. Then basketball season started. With freshman LeBron, the team never lost. The team even won a state title. And he was just getting started.

By his junior year, LeBron was dominant. He was 6-foot-7 and strong. Opponents struggled to keep up with him. Thousands of people came to his games. This included NBA **scouts**. Some believed he was already ready for the NBA. But LeBron still had one more year of high school.

LeBron quit football for his senior year. By then his basketball skills were famous. Some of his games were even shown on ESPN. LeBron ended high school with a third state title. Then it was on to the NBA Draft. His hometown team, the Cleveland Cavaliers, picked him first overall.

The Cavaliers selected LeBron first overall in the 2003 NBA Draft.

FUN FACT

In February 2002, *Sports Illustrated* put LeBron on its cover, calling him "The Chosen One."

LeBron goes up for a shot during his senior year of high school.

CHAPTER 3

Using His Platform

The phone rings. A young boy answers. He can't believe who's calling.

"Hey, it's LeBron."

The message is recorded. But that's because James needs to call a lot of kids.

"I got a very special message today," James continues, "letting me know what a great job you did in school. I'm so proud of you guys."

Students in Akron, Ohio, received this message. It came after school one day. These students were part of James's **foundation**. He sends these messages to encourage them.

Growing up in Akron, James had a lot of challenges. He knows kids there face similar challenges. Now James wants to help them. He does that through his foundation.

James rides bikes with kids during a fundraiser.

James speaks at the opening of the I Promise School in 2018.

Students arrive for school. Teachers greet them in the hallways. They hug and high-five each student. The song "We Are Family" plays. The teachers dance. They want the students to be excited about going to school.

James created his foundation. Then he started an entire school. The I Promise School opened in 2018. It's in Akron. James had a hard childhood. So do these students. James is trying to help them. The school has special programs. It's also free. The foundation pays for it. It will also pay for students to attend the University of Akron.

James and his family in 2018.

FUN FACT

James met his wife, Savannah, in high school. They married in 2013 and have three children.

James settles into a chair. He leans back. Then he begins chatting. James appears to be in a barbershop. But he's actually on a TV show. Football stars Odell Beckham Jr. and Michael Bennett join him. The show is called *The Shop*. Different celebrities join James. They discuss many topics.

Basketball helped make James famous. Then he became even more famous. James has been in many shows and movies. He has hosted *Saturday Night Live*. He also played himself in the movie *Trainwreck*. James now helps start TV shows such as *The Shop*. He has also created **documentaries**.

FUN FACT
Only five pro athletes made more money than James in 2018.

James walks the red carpet at a movie premiere.

CAREER TIMELINE

1984

December 30, 1984
LeBron James is born in Akron, Ohio.

2003

June 26, 2003
The Cleveland Cavaliers take James with the first pick in the 2003 NBA Draft.

2007

June 7, 2007
James plays in his first NBA Finals game against the San Antonio Spurs. The Spurs go on to defeat the Cavaliers in four games.

2010

July 8, 2010
In a TV special, James announces he is leaving Cleveland to play for the Miami Heat.

2012

June 21, 2012
James wins his first NBA championship with the Heat. They defeat the Oklahoma City Thunder in five games.

2014

July 10, 2014
After four seasons in Miami, James announces he's returning to his home state to again play for Cleveland.

2016

June 19, 2016
James leads the way as the Cavaliers defeat the Golden State Warriors in the NBA Finals. It's the first time in 52 years a major pro sports team from Cleveland has won a championship.

2018

May 27, 2018
James and the Cavaliers go to the NBA Finals. James becomes the fifth player in NBA history to make eight consecutive NBA Finals.

2018

July 9, 2018
The Los Angeles Lakers sign James to a four-year contract.

CHAPTER 4

Years of Success

LeBron James shoots. Swish! Then he shoots again. Another basket! James keeps shooting. And he keeps scoring. No one on the Detroit Pistons can stop him.

James was only in his fourth NBA season in the spring of 2007. His Cleveland Cavaliers were a team on the rise. But most expected them to fall to Detroit in the playoffs. James made sure that didn't happen. He scored 29 of his team's last 30 points. The Cavs won. And the win sent them to the NBA Finals.

The amazing run ended there. The San Antonio Spurs had a lot of experience. They easily beat Cleveland. But James was just twenty-two. His future looked bright.

Cleveland, Ohio

FUN FACT
James made every NBA All-Star Game from 2005 through 2019.

James was practically unstoppable against the Pistons in Game 5 of the 2007 Eastern Conference finals.

In 2010, Cleveland fans started booing James. Earlier that year he became a **free agent**. He joined the Miami Heat. Cavaliers fans were mad. They thought he turned his back on his hometown team.

James finally won his first championship in 2012 with the Heat.

James wanted to try something new. He also wanted to play with his friends Dwyane Wade and Chris Bosh. All three were All-Stars. Fans called the Heat a "superteam." They lived up to the name. Miami reached the NBA Finals four years in a row. It won in 2012 and 2013. James was a huge star. Then he was ready for something different. In 2014, he decided to go back to Cleveland.

THE DECISION

By 2010, James was a superstar. Every team wanted to sign him. He decided to announce his choice on ESPN. The show was called "The Decision." However, the show angered many people. They thought James was disrespectful to Cleveland.

James introduces himself to Miami Heat fans after signing with the team in 2010.

James has unique skills. He is big and strong. He can shoot well. He is also a great dribbler and defender. And he is smart. In Miami, James had finally become an NBA champion.

Now he wanted to make Cleveland a champion. In 2016, he did just that. James was a local hero again. He tried hard to win another championship. The team reached four NBA Finals in a row. But it only won in 2016.

By 2018, James was ready for another change. That summer he joined the Los Angeles Lakers. They are a famous team. James was ready to be part of that history.

James hoped to build on his legacy by joining the Lakers.

CAREER

STATS

Through the 2018-19 season

GAMES PLAYED	1,198
POINTS PER GAME	27.2
REBOUNDS PER GAME	7.4
ASSISTS PER GAME	7.2
SHOOTING PERCENTAGE	.504

BEYOND

THE BOOK

After reading the book, it's time to think about what you learned. Try the following exercises to jumpstart your ideas.

THINK

THAT'S NEWS TO ME. James helped his hometown Cleveland Cavaliers to the NBA championship in 2016. How might news sources be able to fill in more detail about this? What new information could you find in news articles? Where could you go to find those sources?

CREATE

SHARPEN YOUR RESEARCH SKILLS. James was popular as a high school basketball player. Where could you go in the library to find more information about his high school basketball career? Who could you talk to who might know more? Create a research plan. Write a paragraph about your next steps.

SHARE

SUM IT UP. Write one paragraph summarizing the important points from this book. Make sure it's in your own words. Don't just copy what is in the text. Share the paragraph with a classmate. What comments does your classmate have about your summary? What additional questions does he or she have about James?

GROW

REAL-LIFE RESEARCH. What places could you visit to learn more about James? What other things could you learn while you were there?

RESEARCH NINJA

Visit *www.ninjaresearcher.com/0417* to learn how to take your research skills and book report writing to the next level!

RESEARCH

DIGITAL LITERACY TOOLS

SEARCH LIKE A PRO
Learn about how to use search engines to find useful websites.

FACT OR FAKE?
Discover how you can tell a trusted website from an untrustworthy resource.

TEXT DETECTIVE
Explore how to zero in on the information you need most.

SHOW YOUR WORK
Research responsibly—learn how to cite sources.

WRITE

GET TO THE POINT
Learn how to express your main ideas.

PLAN OF ATTACK
Learn prewriting exercises and create an outline.

DOWNLOADABLE REPORT FORMS

Further Resources

BOOKS

Kortemeier, Todd. *It's Great to be a Fan in Ohio.* Focus Readers, 2019.

Levit, Joseph. *Basketball's G. O. A. T.: Michael Jordan, LeBron James, and More.* Lerner Publications, 2020.

Payment, Simone. *LeBron James*. Rosen Central, 2019.

WEBSITES

FACTSURFER

Factsurfer.com gives you a safe, fun way to find more information.

1. Go to www.factsurfer.com.
2. Enter "LeBron James" into the search box and click 🔍.
3. Select your book cover to see a list of related websites.

Glossary

backboard: A backboard is the board behind the basket where the ball might bounce off. James blocked a shot off the backboard in the 2016 NBA Finals.

documentaries: Documentaries are movies that show real-life stories. James helped make documentaries about basketball players.

draft: Pro sports teams use a draft to choose new players to add to their rosters. The Cleveland Cavaliers selected James with the first pick in the 2003 draft.

foundation: A foundation is an organization that helps people in need. James created a foundation to support kids in Akron, Ohio.

free agent: A free agent is an athlete who can sign with any team. James was a free agent when he joined the Miami Heat.

free throws: Basketball players shoot free throws when they are fouled. James hit two free throws to put the Los Angeles Lakers ahead.

rebound: A basketball player gets a rebound when he or she gets the ball after a missed shot. James brought down the rebound and started his team on offense.

scouts: Scouts are people who watch other teams and players to get more information about them. Many scouts went out to watch James play high school basketball.

Index

PHOTO CREDITS

The images in this book are reproduced through the courtesy of: Michael Conroy/AP Images, front cover (center); Chris Szagola/AP Images, front cover (right), p. 3; Torsak Thammachote/Shutterstock Images, front cover (background bottom); Oleksii Sidorov/Shutterstock Images, front cover (background top); Marcio Jose Sanchez/AP Images, pp. 4–5, 26; Eric Risberg/AP Images, p. 6, 9; Tony Dejak/AP Images, pp. 7, 14; Red Line Editorial, pp. 8, 21, 27 (chart); Ron Schwane/AP Images, pp. 10–11; Henryk Sadura/Shutterstock Images, pp. 12–13; freestyle images/Shutterstock Images, p. 13; Bruce Schwartzman/AP Images, p. 15; Phil Long/AP Images, pp. 16–17, 18; Kathy Hutchins/Shutterstock Images, pp. 19, 20; Steven R Smith/Shutterstock Images, p. 22; Paul Sancya/AP Images, p. 23; Lynne Sladky/AP Images, p. 24; J.Pat Carter/AP Images, p. 25; Mark J. Terrill/AP Images, p. 27 (LeBron James); Cherdchai charasri/Shutterstock Images, p. 30.

ABOUT THE AUTHOR

Anthony K. Hewson is a freelance writer originally from San Diego, now living in the Bay Area with his wife and their two dogs.